Disney
PUPPY DOG PALS

Design-a-Dog

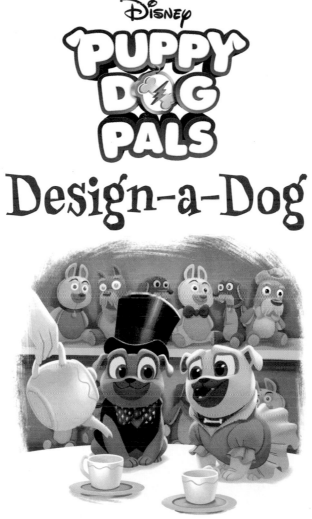

ADAPTED BY **MICHAEL OLSON**

BASED ON THE EPISODE WRITTEN BY **JESSICA CARLETON**

FOR THE SERIES CREATED BY **HARLAND WILLIAMS**

ILLUSTRATED BY THE **DISNEY STORYBOOK ART TEAM**

Disney PRESS

Los Angeles · New York

Bingo and Rolly are curled up on the couch, watching their favorite show. "*Captain Dog* will be back after these messages," says the announcer.

"How would you like to build your own stuffed animal, dress it up, and take it home to play?" the lady in the commercial says.

"I would LOVE that!" Bingo declares.
The puppies sing along to the ad:

"Come to Design-a-Dog today!"

Later that day, Bob walks downstairs, carrying a box of old toys. "I had tons of fun with these toys, but it's time someone else got to have fun with them," he says. Bob sets down the box and heads to work.

A box FULL of toys? Bingo and Rolly cannot wait to see what's inside!

The first thing the puppies find is a worn old stuffed dog.
"I like this thing!" says Rolly. "It's shakity-shakey!"
Bingo wants to shake it, too. The puppies each grab one end of
the toy and shake. Suddenly . . . RIIP! Stuffing flies everywhere!

"You just ruined Ruff-Ruff!" Hissy exclaims. "He was Bob's favorite toy when he was a kid."

"Then it's our mission to fix him," Bingo says. "And I know just where to go!"

The puppies rush to their doghouse for their special collars and then head out.

MISSION: FIX RUFF-RUFF

Bingo and Rolly take Ruff-Ruff to Design-a-Dog. The store is filled with stuffed dogs of every size, shape, and color. Three big machines make sure each toy is stuffed, sewn, and groomed. Bingo and Rolly spot the lady from the commercial talking to some children.

"Follow those kids!"

Rolly says.

First the lady shows the kids the stuffing machine. "After you pick out your toy doggy, you put it in here to get stuffed," she says. "And when it's done, it will come out here—a perfectly poufy pooch!"

Once the lady walks away, the puppies hop inside the
machine. They hook up the stuffing hose to fill Ruff-Ruff
till he's a perfectly poufy pooch.

Ruff-Ruff gets stuffed with more and more fluff, until . . .

. . . the hose comes loose!
"Stuffing storm!" the puppies shout excitedly.

Next the lady shows the kids the sewing machine.

A girl named Chloe sits down and powers the sewing machine by pressing the pedals with her feet. "This is fun!" she says, giggling.

When the kids move on, the puppies put Ruff-Ruff inside the sewing machine and jump onto the pedals.

Bingo says, "When I go up, up, up, you go—"

"Down, down, down!" Rolly shouts as they sew Ruff-Ruff.

The last machine is the grooming machine. "First we get the doggies clean," the lady explains. "Then we give them some style, and then some bling!"

"Let's get Ruff-Ruff cleaned, styled, and blinged before we take him back to Bob," says Bingo. "And we might as well get ourselves looking good, too!"

The puppies leap into the grooming machine with Ruff-Ruff. Brushes and blow-dryers clean, style, and bling up Ruff-Ruff and the pups.

"We did it!"

Bingo says. "Ruff-Ruff looks better than ever!"
"And we look pretty pup-tacular ourselves," declares Rolly.

The pups are ready to get Ruff-Ruff home when they see the lady heading toward them. "It's time for a tea-pup party!" she says. The kids scurry over to choose a toy to play with.

"This one is my favorite," Chloe says, picking up Ruff-Ruff.

"I want two," says another girl, grabbing Bingo and Rolly.

The pugs don't know what else to do—so they freeze! The girl dresses them in costumes and makes them drink pretend tea.

"There's nothing in the cup," Rolly whispers to Bingo. "I'm still thirsty!"

Next it's time for the Design-a-Dog
roller-skating sing-along.

"Whoaaaa!"

Rolly calls, slipping and sliding on his skates.

Finally, it's time for the kids to pick out toy puppies to take home. Chloe
is just about to choose Ruff-Ruff!

"We need to grab Ruff-Ruff and get out of here!" Bingo says.

Bingo and Rolly skate toward the pile of toy puppies as fast as they can.

Suddenly, Rolly loses control and slides into a display with a **CRASH!**
Chloe turns around, giving Bingo just enough time to jump into
the pile of toys, grab Ruff-Ruff, and go!

Back home at last, Bingo and Rolly show off Ruff-Ruff's makeover.

"This thing looks amazing!" says Hissy.

"Yup! Bob won't even know we took it out of the box," Bingo says.

Just then, Bob walks in the front door. After he greets his pets, he takes the box of toys outside for the donation center to pick up.

As Bob sets down the box, Chloe and her mom walk by.
"That looks like the doggy from the store!" Chloe exclaims.
"How would you like to keep him?" Bob asks with a smile.
Rolly turns to Bingo. "Bob is happy, and so is Chloe!"
"Mission accomplished," Bingo says. **"High paw!"**